CRANKENSTEIN

WRITTEN by
SAMANTHA BERGER

ILLUSTRATED by
DAN SANTAT

LITTLE, BROWN AND COMPANY
NEW YORK   BOSTON

HAVE YOU SEEN CRANKENSTEIN?

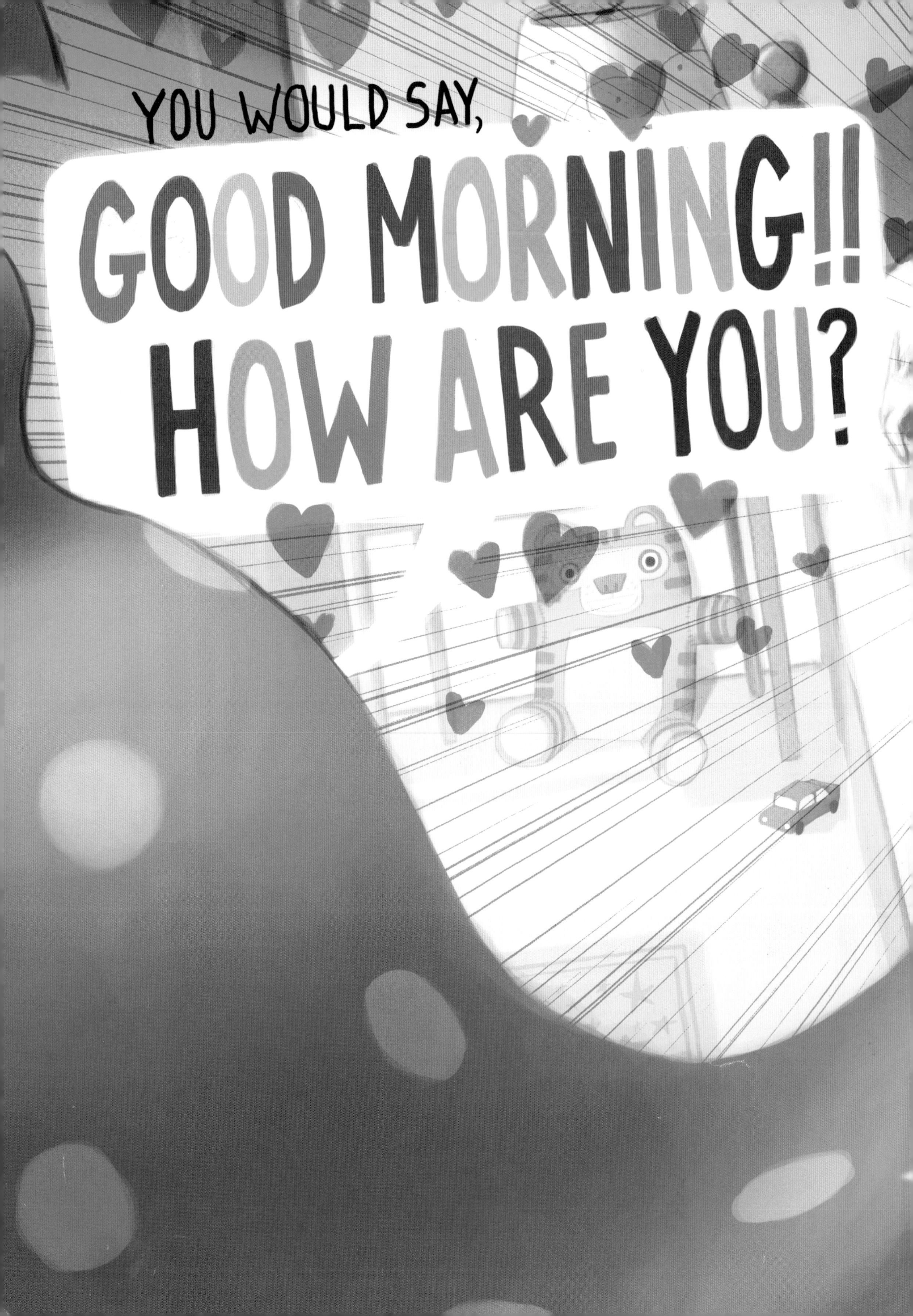
YOU WOULD SAY,
GOOD MORNING!!
HOW ARE YOU?

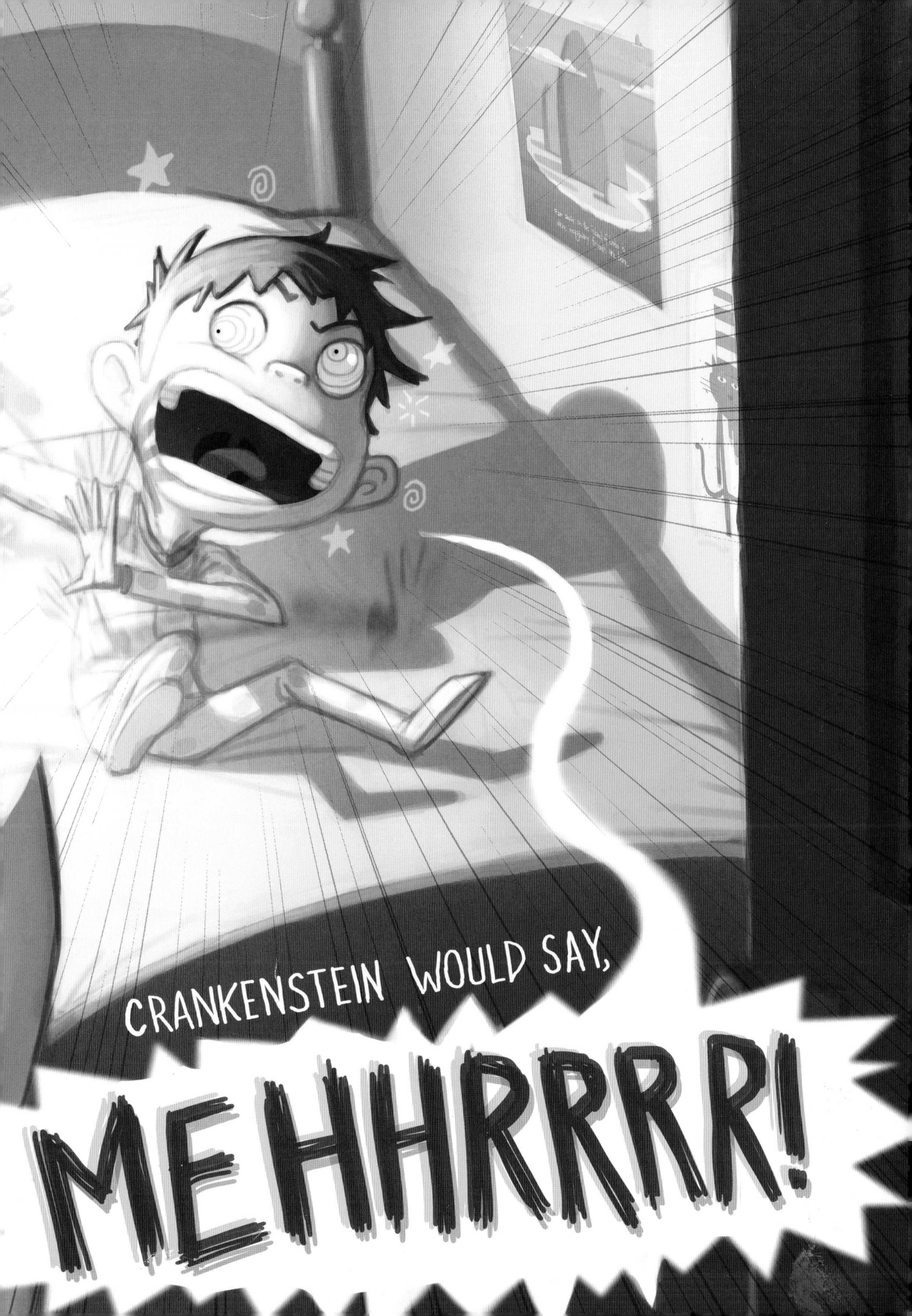
CRANKENSTEIN WOULD SAY,
MEHHRRRR!

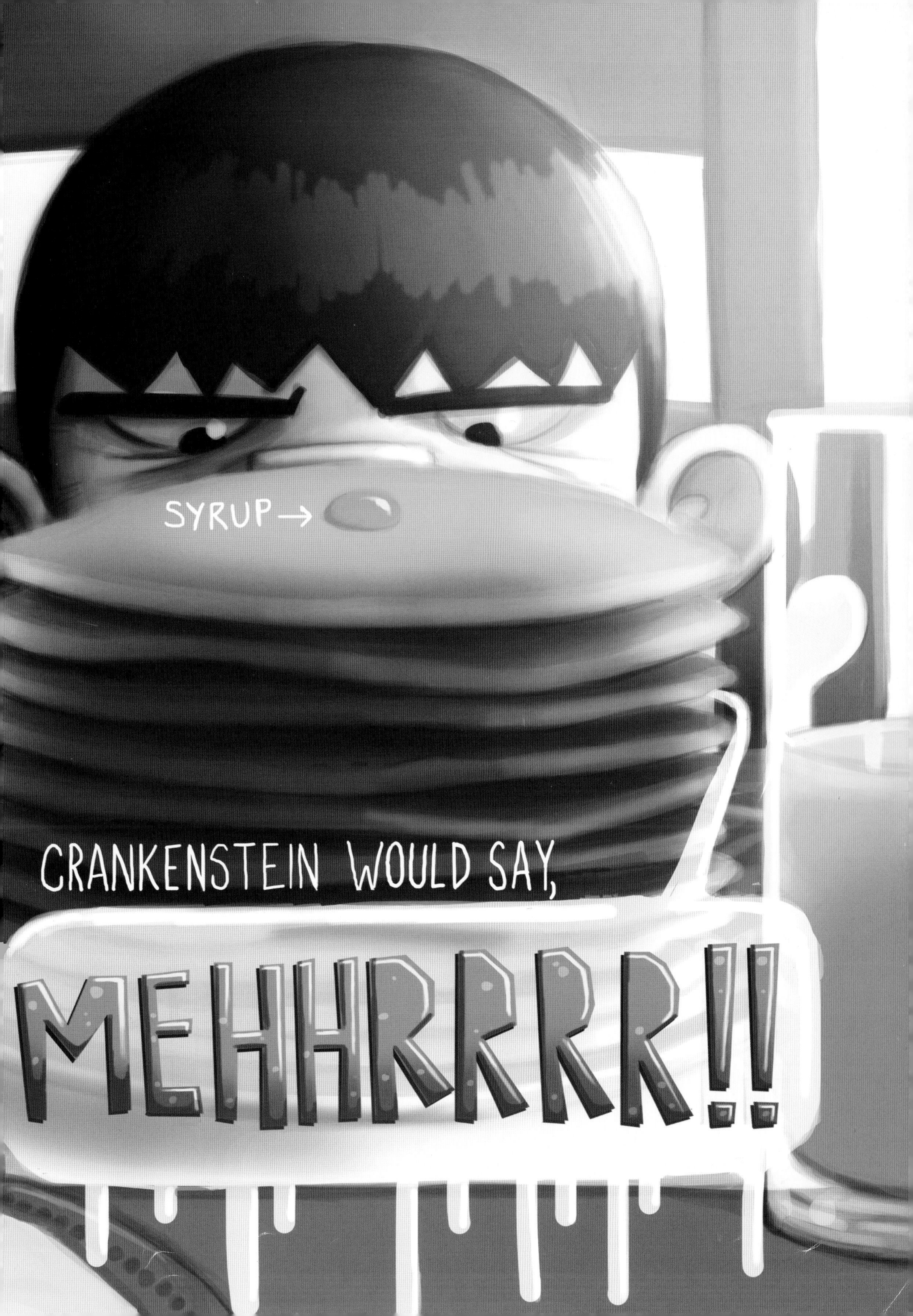
SYRUP→
CRANKENSTEIN WOULD SAY,
MEHHRRRR!!

YOU WOULD SAY,

TIME FOR

SCHOOL!

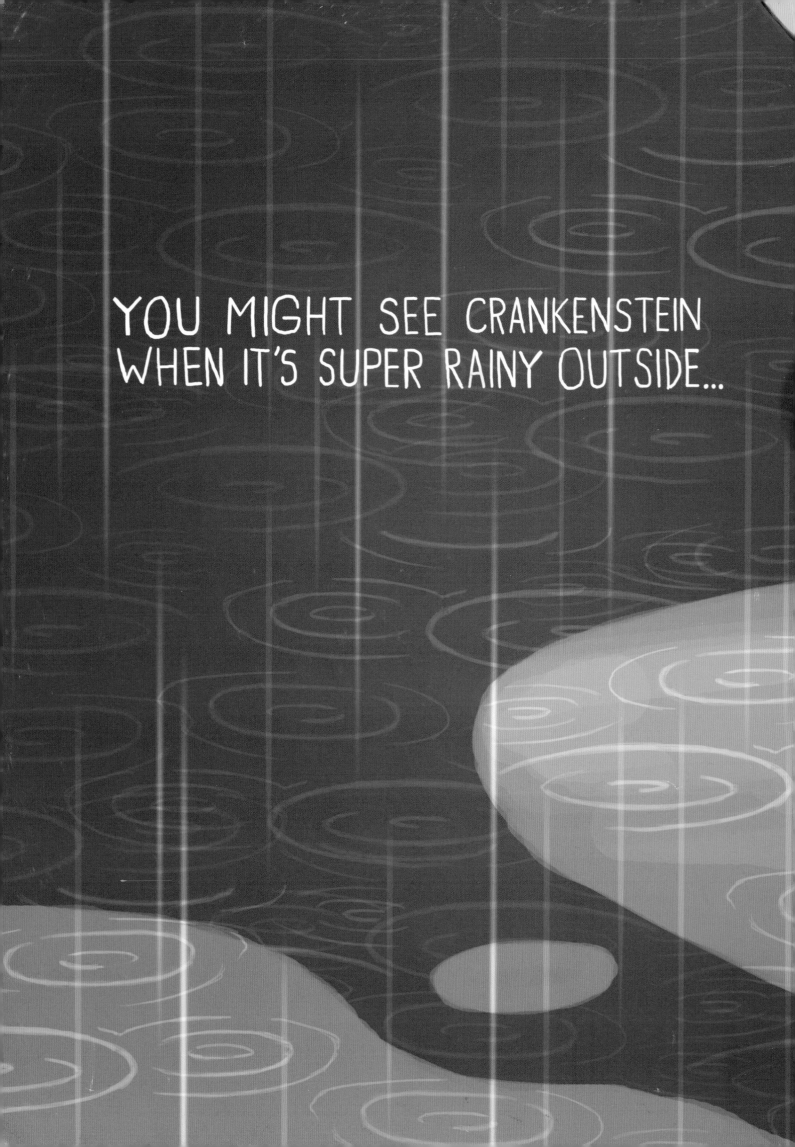

OR WHEN IT'S EXTRA COLD ON HALLOWEEN...

OR WHEN IT'S **WAY** TOO HOT FOR POPSICLES.

MEHHHRRRR!!!

ESPECIALLY WHEN IT'S WAY TOO HOT FOR POPSICLES.

CRANKENSTEIN *HATES* LONG, LONG LINES.

CRANKENSTEIN *HATES*
GROSS COUGH SYRUP.

CRANKENSTEIN *HATES* WHEN
YOU SAY IT'S BEDTIME.

MEHHRRR!

YES, THAT CRANKENSTEIN IS SOME PRETTY
SCARY BUSINESS, ALL RIGHT.

BUT JUST WHEN YOU THINK THAT MONSTER IS HERE TO STAY...

MEH?

HE MIGHT DO SOMETHING
THAT SURPRISES YOU.
BECAUSE WHEN CRANKENSTEIN
MEETS *ANOTHER* CRANKENSTEIN...

LAUGH.

...AT LEAST FOR NOW.

...BUT DEFINITELY NOT TODAY.